The Talking Bird and the Story Pouch

The

Talking Bird

and the

Story Pouch

BY AMY LAWSON

ILLUSTRATED BY CRAIG McFARLAND BROWN

HARPER & ROW, PUBLISHERS

The Talking Bird and the Story Pouch
Text copyright © 1987 by Amy Lawson
Illustrations copyright © 1987 by Craig McFarland Brown
Printed in the United States of America. For
information address Harper & Row Junior Books, 10
East 53rd Street, New York, N.Y. 10022. Published
simultaneously in Canada by Fitzhenry & Whiteside
Limited, Toronto.
Designed by Trish Parcell
10 9 8 7 6 5 4 3 2 1
First Edition

Library of Congress Cataloging-in-Publication Data
Lawson, Amy.
      The talking bird and the story pouch.

      Summary: Storyteller, whose calling has been passed
down to him from a long line of storytellers, looks for
stories everywhere until a magical adventure to Blue
Mountain teaches him that his storytelling powers are
within himself.
      [1. Storytelling—Fiction.   2. Self-perception—
Fiction]   I. Brown, Craig McFarland, ill.   II. Title.
PZ7.L438228Tal 1987   [Fic]   86-45493
ISBN 0-06-023833-X
ISBN 0-06-023834-8 (lib. bdg.)

*For Richard, who helped me find my stories
and Jan, who helped me shape them.*

The Talking Bird and the Story Pouch

Once upon a time in the land between the Sea and Blue Mountain, when the Great-Grandfather was a boy, he walked in the forest searching for crinkleroot and black mica, for winterberries and owls' feathers.

One day, as he looked down at the forest floor, his eye was caught by a polished circle of wood.

No larger than the palm of his hand, the circle was smooth on one side, carved with the figure of a bird on the other.

"A heron with its bill open wide," observed the Great-Grandfather, tracing the carving with his fingers.

The Great-Grandfather hung the bird around his neck. Before long, he discovered he could find not only birds' feathers and sweet-tasting berries, but he could also find stories. He found them in the lights and shadows of the stones and streams, in the bark of trees, under boulders in the fields.

"I expect the carving is a charm to help me find stories," said the Great-Grandfather. "I shall wear it always and call it the Talking Bird."

So it was that the Great-Grandfather became a storyteller.

With magic he learned from *his* great-grandfather, the Great-Grandfather sewed a story pouch of beaver, mink, and otter. When he told a story, his words knit together and dropped into the pouch. Of course he could remember his own stories, but now he would be able to pass them on to his son.

In time, the son wore the Talking Bird and carried the Story Pouch, searching through the forest for his own stories.

So it was that the Grandfather became a storyteller.

And, in time, he had a son who became a storyteller.

And by and by, *he* had a son.

How soft the leather felt in the boy's hands, and how smooth the wood of the Talking Bird, which had been polished by so many fingers.

But while the boy grew and learned all the stories that had been found so far, he really preferred to fish through the streams of the forest for stickleback and mud minnows, mooneyes and trout perch.

And so it was the boy became a storyteller . . . sort of.

The Storyteller and his Wise Old Mother and Cat lived in a log cabin.

The surrounding trees were tall and thick trunked. Their bark was rough and deeply grooved like the Storyteller's mother's face. A stream ran by, and a stone wall. The boulders of the wall were of all shapes and sizes, falling every which way.

The Storyteller walked with the open Story Pouch slung over his shoulder, the Talking Bird charm around his neck. As soon as he found a story, he told it to the sky, and the words knit together, dropping neatly into the pouch. The Cat followed nearby, stalking voles.

"Cat," said the Storyteller, closing up the mouth of the Story Pouch, "who is to say that a Storyteller, once he has found a story or two, cannot go fishing?"

"The truth is," observed the Cat, "when he catches a fish, he doesn't have to tell it."

The Storyteller spent some time every day gathering stories because that was what his father and grandfather and great-grandfather had done, but he did not like to tell them. The ones he found were not as good as the ones he had learned from the Story Pouch. No one would want to hear them.

The Wise Old Mother did not exactly know this, but she was suspicious. She could not understand why her son was not, as his father had been, and his father, and *his* father, the greatest storyteller in the land between the Sea and Blue Mountain.

One evening, the Wise Old Mother told the Storyteller he needed a horse.

"I don't need a horse," said the Storyteller, who was afraid of horses.

"You do," said the Wise Old Mother as she swept the cabin

with her corn-husk broom. "For traveling far and wide. You need to find some new stories, so that you can become the greatest storyteller in the land between the Sea and Blue Mountain."

"One good old story is better than twenty new bad ones," grumbled the Storyteller, skipping out of her way. He could tell by her broom stabbing that he was in for a long evening's scold. "And besides, who says I want to be the greatest storyteller in the land between the Sea and Blue Mountain?"

"Have you no pride?" The Wise Old Mother's voice trembled as she hung up the broom. She stirred a porridge pot over the fire. "Why do you think," she asked, "your father passed on the Story Pouch and the Talking Bird? So you could sit around and fish? Sometimes I am not even sure you are *telling* your stories."

Even the knots in the floor stared up at the Storyteller with accusing little eyeballs.

"Sit down and eat your supper," commanded the Wise Old Mother, slapping a bowl on the table.

The Storyteller sat down. The Wise Old Mother sat down with him so as to be more comfortable for close-in suppertime scolding.

"Someday you are going to lose the Talking Bird," contin-

ued the Wise Old Mother. "Then how will you find your stories, Storyteller, tell me that?" The Storyteller twisted a hole in his porridge with his spoon. "I suppose now you are going to tell me you do not even want to be a storyteller."

The Storyteller scooped up a mountain of porridge with his spoon. "I like storytelling," he said. "Just not all the time."

"Oh," said the Wise Old Mother with a little scream, "if your father and his father and *his* father could only hear you."

"I think," said the Storyteller, rising slowly from the table, "you may be right. Perhaps I will look for a horse. This very minute."

The Cat, who was warming himself by the fireplace, rubbed a paw thoughtfully across his whiskers. The Wise Old Mother breathed out an unused scolding breath.

"This very minute?" she asked. "It's dark outside."

"This very minute," said the Storyteller in his loudest lying tone of voice. "I'll take my torch."

"Try to find a horse that isn't too worn," said the Wise Old Mother as he went to the peg for his hat and Story Pouch. "And check his gums. Black specks mean a bad liver, and that means he'll laugh at his own jokes."

"Don't wait up for me," said the Storyteller, waving cheerfully with the torch. "I don't know when I'll be back."

"Not sure you'd better come back," said the Wise Old Mother with a sniff. She dumped his porridge into the fire. "If he comes back with a horse, I'll not scold for a week."

"If he comes back with a horse, I'll give up voles for a week," said the Cat. "But," he said, slipping out the door, "I'll just keep an eye on him."

The Storyteller ambled through the old, old forest where the trees were tall and thick trunked. Sighing, he sat on one of the boulders of a stone wall.

"All I wanted," he said, "was to get away from a long evening's scold, but now I have to go look for a horse. However," he said, "perhaps I had better catch a fish first. After all, I did not eat any supper."

The Storyteller walked to his favorite fishing spot, where fragrant ferns scented the air.

"Now," he said, sitting on the bank and pulling a line and fishhook from the pouch, "now for some peace and quiet."

The Storyteller closed his eyes. The Cat, who had been following, curled up behind a boulder and went to sleep.

For a long time, it was still and quiet in the old, old forest except for the occasional quawk of a night heron.

A fish jumped, startling the Storyteller's eyes wide open.

Splunk! The fish jumped again, but this time the Storyteller saw that it was not a fish. At least, he had never before seen a fish with rabbit ears. "Perhaps I did not see what I saw," he considered.

Two rabbit ears rose out of the water, followed by two eyes that reflected the torchlight.

The creature swam with effort toward the Storyteller. It heaved, seal-like, up on the bank. As it came to rest, its belly sagged over the Storyteller's foot.

"Oooooooooooof!" said the creature.

"Mmmmmmmmmmmmmmm," said the Storyteller.

"How do you do?" asked the creature, politely extending a flipper. "I'm the Kulloo Makoo." Water dripped from its flipper down the Storyteller's neck.

"If I close my eyes," said the Cat, who was now awake and hiding behind the boulder, "maybe it will go away."

"Do tell a story," said the Kulloo Makoo. It had a sticky maple-syrup sort of voice. Its belly billowed in and out as it caught its breath. "Even though I have just eaten a pouchful of stories, I am still hungry."

The Storyteller opened his eyes very wide. He was startled

to see himself reflected in the Kulloo Makoo's round black eyes.

"Hungry?" asked the Storyteller.

"Hun-gry," repeated the Kulloo Makoo, "for stories. Your stories. Yum," he added, smacking his lips and rubbing his belly.

"Where did you find my stories?" asked the Storyteller, not quite believing the Kulloo Makoo.

"In your pouch," said the Kulloo Makoo. "It was lying open on the bank. I didn't think you'd mind."

The Storyteller reached for the Story Pouch. He stuck in two fingers and pulled out two pieces of old grass.

"My stories!" cried the Storyteller. "You have been eating *my* stories?" His own surprised faces stared at him from out of the Kulloo Makoo's eyes. "And not only my stories, but my father's, and his father's, and *his* father's stories."

"I'm sorry," said the Kulloo Makoo. His eyes clouded so the Storyteller could no longer see himself. "But what am I to do? A Kulloo Makoo eats stories. The ones from your pouch were very good, but," continued the Kulloo Makoo, "it would be much easier to eat the words right out of your mouth. Perhaps you could find me a nice juicy one? After all, I came all the way from the Sea just to hear you." He glanced at the Storyteller and then cast his eyes shyly down at his flippers.

The Storyteller twisted a finger around and around in his beard. He chewed on a twig. He tugged at the Talking Bird around his neck. He was thinking hard.

"Tell you what," said the Storyteller after a long silence. "Since you like my stories so much, I will give you the greatest story ever told by a Storyteller. It is so precious I have never before dared tell it."

"What can he be thinking of?" murmured the Cat. "The Storyteller has never before told *any* story."

"How wonderfully kind you are," sighed the Kulloo Makoo. He plumped his back up against the bank and folded his flippers over his belly. "Once upon a time," he started eagerly. "Isn't that how all your stories begin?"

The Storyteller nodded. "Once upon a time," he said, his eyes as sharp as needles. "Once upon an ever-so-distant time," he added, making sure the Story Pouch was tightly closed. The Kulloo Makoo made a breeze by wagging his ears so the Storyteller's words would drift into his mouth.

"When the world was very, very, very, very, very young," continued the Storyteller, "and the sea and the stars and the moon and the trees and the sand and the grass and the whales and the wheat and the hares and the seals and the blackbirds, blackberries, and bluebirds, and the goldfinch, goldenrod, and goldfish..."

"Pardon me," said the Kulloo Makoo, nervously noting the expression on the Storyteller's face, "I am getting filled up rather fast on all these words."

The Storyteller picked up a stick and poked the Kulloo Makoo in the soft part of his belly. "Don't you—" and he poked again—"ever interrupt while I'm telling the greatest story of all time."

"I'm sorry," murmured the Kulloo Makoo, tears welling. "Please go on."

"...and the leaves and the ladybugs," continued the Storyteller, "and the sparrows and the yarrows and the moths and the mists," and the Storyteller went on, feeding the Kulloo Makoo word after word after word. Every time the Kulloo Makoo tried to raise a flipper to stop him, the Storyteller poked him in the belly.

"Oooooooooog!" groaned the Kulloo Makoo when the night was half over. "Oooooooooooh! Please, Storyteller, please, stop! No more! If I eat another word I shall burst."

"What!" cried the Storyteller. "How can any creature be as

ill-mannered as you?" He held up the stick as if it were the staff of a king. "And what," he asked, "will you give me if I promise not to go on with the greatest story of all time?"

The Kulloo Makoo tried to sit up, but all he could do was feebly lift his face up out of his chins.

"My tummy hurts so much," he groaned. "I will give you anything."

"Clever, clever Storyteller," said the Cat, poking his head above the boulder.

The Storyteller flung down his stick. "THEN GIVE ME BACK MY STORIES," he roared. "How can I pass on my stories if I don't have stories to pass on?"

"Ohhhhh," moaned the Kulloo Makoo, covering his eyes with his ears. "I want to give back your stories, but I—"

"—and maples and magpies and foxes and fir trees and . . ."

"STOP!" cried the Kulloo Makoo. "I will give back your stories. It is just that I cannot simply give them to you. I must *tell* them to you."

The Storyteller carefully placed the pouch on the ground with its mouth open toward the Kulloo Makoo. "Start telling," he commanded.

"Once upon a time," started the Kulloo Makoo, and he told

the Storyteller's stories and his father's stories, and his father's, and *his* father's, from that moment until dawn, and from that dawn until the next day.

"I have found some pretty good stories after all," said the Storyteller in surprise. He had never heard his stories told by anyone but himself. "One or two are even as good as my father's," he added, with a new prickly feeling of pride.

When the Kulloo Makoo finally said, "And so the story ends," for the last time, he fainted and rolled into the water. He would have drowned if the Storyteller had not pulled him out and pumped his belly.

"Now go back to the Sea where you belong," said the Storyteller severely.

"Back to the same old boring fish stories," sighed the Kulloo Makoo. "Good-bye, Storyteller."

"Wait!" cried the Storyteller, feeling sorry for the Kulloo Makoo. He tugged at the Talking Bird as he looked thoughtfully into the water. "I think I see a story," he said. "If you are not greedy, but chew slowly, it may last you on your journey home."

"Oh, Storyteller!" cried the Kulloo Makoo, clapping his flippers joyfully together.

"Sit still," growled the Cat. "He has never before told a story to anyone but the sky."

"Are you ready?" asked the Storyteller, feeling a little nervous. He closed up the pouch again to keep the words from going into it instead of the Kulloo Makoo.

Once upon a time [he said], *there was a boy who lived by the sea. Every day he went to a beach that was uncovered by the tide when all the other beaches were covered. There he would throw a handful of smooth white pebbles into the water and cry, "Wishes, wishes, turn to fishes." Every day those pebbles grew fins and gills, scales and tails. The boy scooped them into a net and brought them home to his mother and father and little sister.*

The boy always fished alone, so no one knew of his secret until, one day, his sister grew old enough to follow him. She watched him throw the pebbles into the sea and cry, "Wishes, wishes, turn to fishes." She watched the pebbles grow fins and gills, scales and tails.

The next day, the boy's sister came with a net. She hid until the boy left with his catch. Then she ran to the beach, threw out a handful of pebbles, and shouted the magic words.

"It works!" she cried as she watched the pebbles grow into fish.

Again and again she scooped pebbles into the sea, shouting the magic louder and louder. Soon the water boiled with the swimming of hundreds of fish.

The girl's shouting brought the boy running to the beach. When he arrived, what a sight he beheld! His sister was squirming on the beach, growing fins and gills, growing scales and a tail.

"Help!" she cried as her lips began to pucker. "You must help me!"

The boy dragged his fish-sister into the water so she could breathe.

"Fish, fish, become my wish," he called, hoping the backward magic would give the girl back her human form. But as the boy watched, a smooth white rock grew up out of the sea in place of the fish.

In time seals gathered there, and sea gulls. And so the story ends.

"Watch out, Kulloo Makoo," said the Cat from on top of the boulder, "that might happen to you if you continue to be so greedy."

The Kulloo Makoo rolled toward the stream. "Thank you,

Storyteller," he cried, splashing noisily into the water. "Thank you, thank you, thank you."

"Stop it," said the Storyteller backing away. "You are getting me wet. Now go away."

The Kulloo Makoo's torchlit eyes flashed above the water, then ears, eyes, and Kulloo Makoo disappeared.

"Telling stories is tiring," said the Storyteller, resting on the bank. "I will go to sleep." Suddenly he sat up. "But he liked it!" he shouted. "The Kulloo Makoo liked my story! Perhaps I will go traveling far and wide to find new stories. After all, I *am* a storyteller."

"I shall go to Blue Mountain," said the Storyteller as he woke up. "My father always told me the best stories were to be found there. But," he added, "that means I really will have to find a horse. Unless," he said, jumping to his feet, "I fell a tree and make a boat. Then I can travel up the stream to the river right to the base of Blue Mountain." He slapped at a mosquito. "A boat's better than a horse, because while you're traveling you can fish."

"Truth is," said the Cat, perched nearby on the stone wall, "boats don't kick."

The Storyteller looked about him for a suitable tree. On the other side of the wall was a flowering crab apple. It was old. The branches were gnarled. It seemed wise, as if it had lived forever. It reminded him of his mother.

"That won't do," he muttered. Just the same, he found himself holding the Talking Bird tightly and looking for a story in the weave of the leaves and branches.

"Hmmmmm," he said, squinting, "I see a mane and two ears, a nose, and eyes the color of old bark. I think I have found a story."

Once upon a time [he said, opening the Pouch], *there was a horse who wandered into Farmer Bone's field. Farmer Bone had just beaten his own horse into eternal lameness, so he was pleased when the stranger horse offered to plow his field for free—on one condition.*

"Farmer Bone," said the horse, "you have to shoulder the harness and plow the last row yourself."

Because the work would cost him no oats, Bone quickly agreed and hitched the horse to the plow. He drove him up and down the field, kicking and cussing so hard, an ordinary horse would have gone lame for certain. Nothing seemed to bother this horse. He just took his time, stopping now and then to catch his breath.

By the time they were finished, Bone was so full of wrath he could have furrowed the earth without a plow. As it was, he hitched himself into the harness, declaring, "I'll show that horse just how it's supposed to be done."

Farmer Bone churned up the field, but instead of moving ahead, his feet kept treading the same place over and over again until he dug a hole and disappeared into it.

The horse peered down the hole. "Can't see a thing," he said, "except for a small trickle of water."

The water rose higher and higher, and that is how there came to be a well in Farmer Bone's field. And so the story ends.

"I am not one of your homespun horse stories," said a voice that sounded like the wind whinnying through branches.

The Storyteller stepped backward. He was not used to his stories talking back to him.

"I said I am not one of your horse tales. Horse *tail*, maybe, but not horse *tale*. Har har." The tree trembled with a laugh that sounded like a horse munching carrots. The Cat wrinkled his nose. He did not like trees that laughed at their own jokes.

"I'll tell you a secret," said the voice, "Shall I tell you in a *hoarse* whisper or a *horse* whisper?"

"Don't tell us at all," grumped the Cat.

"I've got wings," continued the voice.

"I can't really see you, or your wings," said the Storyteller.

"Can't see me," snorted the voice. "You probably can't see the nose on your face, either."

"If I shut one eye I can," said the Storyteller, doing so.

"I can see *my* nose clear as oats," said the voice proudly.

"This would make a good story if it weren't happening to me," said the Storyteller.

"I'd come down," said the voice, "but I'm attached to this tree. Mostly it's my tail that's disorganized. Maybe that cat could come up and help."

"Cat," said the Storyteller, seeing him for the first time, "will you?" The Cat yawned, pretending he hadn't heard. "Cat," said the Storyteller sternly.

The Cat slowly clawed up the tree. The branches shook and there was a sound of tearing leaves. "Pah! Horth hair!" spat the Cat.

"You were expecting fur?" asked the voice. "Now then," it said, "thank you very much, Cat, and watch out."

There was a shuddering and quivering of the apple branches. Two clouds of leaves and blossoms tore free of the tree. The Storyteller watched openmouthed as a piebald horse with leafy green wings landed, forelegs first, on the other side of the wall. It winked one of its old bark-colored eyes at the Cat, who was clinging halfway down the tree.

"Hey," said the Horse, nudging the Cat to the ground. "Hey, Cat, what do you call a piebald horse with apple tree wings? An *apple pie*, har har." The Horse laughed a carrot-munching laugh, exposing his gums. They were covered with black specks.

"Ugh, horse breath," said the Cat, arching his back.

"How many flying horses do you know—"

"None," said the Cat rudely.

"—have wings that grow apples," continued the Horse. "Of course, come autumn, the leaves turn and tumble to the ground, but that just keeps me humble. Then I have to walk like everybody else." A smile flickered in his eyes. "The best part, as you can see, is I turn pink in spring. In summer I am a wondrous green." He lowered his head and snorted. "Maybe you would like to know why I don't have true wings? I could tell you the story," he added hopefully.

"Certainly not," said the Cat.

"Yes, please do," said the Storyteller politely. He sat on the stone wall to listen. "It's not often I get to hear other people tell stories."

"Or *tell* other people stories for that matter," murmured the Cat.

"I was born under an apple tree in a modest little meadow," the Horse began. He paused, plucking up a strand of grass to chew. The Cat twitched his ears impatiently. "It was a modest little meadow," repeated the Horse. "Vernal grass with its sweet hay scent. Lovely flowering pale-violet-blue cranesbill. My mother's gentle nosing as she urged me to stand for the first time."

"When do we get to the wings?" asked the Cat.

"But," said the Horse, pulling back his lips into a gummy smile, "it was, as I told you, only a modest little meadow. I set out one May morning to discover greater meadows and greener apple trees. How do you like my story so far?" the Horse asked eagerly.

"Boring," said the Cat.

"Do go on," urged the Storyteller. "If my stories had so many fine words, I am not sure the Story Pouch would be fit to carry them."

The Horse looked down his nose at the Storyteller. "Storytelling, after adventuring, is my greatest skill. Bears come out of hibernation just to hear me."

"Boring," repeated the Cat.

"On the very day I set out," said the Horse, "I received my wondrous wings." He looked over his shoulder and gently rustled the leaves. "Pretty, aren't they? Well," he continued, "I meandered with the river toward Blue Mountain. As I approached a leafy glen, I saw a sight that sent my mane upstanding."

"Huh," said the Cat, rolling his eyes.

"Yes?" said the Storyteller, leaning forward expectantly.

The Horse bit at a bumblebee that hovered about his wings. "Screaming birds were lunging at a woman," he said. "She thrashed her arms wildly, trying to beat them off with a stick. Long scrawny-necked birds they were, with crimson bills in heads as white as bone. They had huge wings that clapped like thunderbolts when they came together."

"Not so boring," said the Cat. "If it's true."

"Most terrifying of all," continued the Horse with a gleam, "were their eyes. They were pools of crackling flame. Having been born brave, I naturally approached. Perhaps, I thought, I

can distract them away from the poor woman. I kicked up my heels, neighed and brayed, and made a wondrous racket. The birds rose like a cloud of giant gnats into the surrounding hemlocks.

"The woman leaned on her stick. 'I'm the Woodcarver,' she said, 'and you have saved me from my own creatures, but only for a moment. I will make you wings and you must lead them away.'

"She touched her stick to an apple tree and cried, 'Now branches be wings!' Two branches broke off and flew to her. She fashioned them across my back. 'Now hurry,' she cried. 'They are coming. Fly, Horse, fly.'

"I broke into a gallop, trying to flap the branches. Soon my hooves struck against air. I rose higher and higher, but it was not long before the birds screamed after me. How could I, a horse, fly faster than these monster birds? I could feel the heat of their fire eyes.

"I turned toward the glistening rock-domed top of a mountain and tumbled upon it, grazing my shanks; for, of course, I had not yet learned to land as gracefully as I do now. The birds followed, pummeling the mountain like hailstones as they landed." The Horse paused to look at his audience.

"Whew," said the Storyteller. "My Story Pouch would never be able to hold such an exciting story."

"No," agreed the Horse. "I daresay that is quite true."

"What happened next?" asked the Storyteller.

"As soon as the birds landed," said the Horse, "their fire eyes dimmed to dull embers and they seemed to fall asleep. So off I flew, swooping and looping and soaring most wondrously. For, after all, how often does a horse get to fly? Unless, of course, he is a *horse*fly, har har."

"Who was the Woodcarver?" asked the Storyteller. "And why were the birds attacking her?"

"Oh," said the Horse, wrinkling his nose. "I don't know."

"You don't know?" asked the Storyteller, bewildered. "At least *my* stories have endings," he said, holding up the Story Pouch.

"It is not my fault," said the Horse with a snort. "I never saw the Woodcarver again. I tried to, but the forest all looks alike when you're flying above it. And believe me," he added, "I keep trying to find her. I need a new pair of wings. Every time I fly too low over an apple tree, I get pulled into it. It is most disconcerting."

"That could be uncomfortable," agreed the Storyteller.

"My search for the Woodcarver never ends," said the Horse. "But maybe," he said, gently nudging the Storyteller, "you'd like to come and help me find her? I do get lonely, and you are a good audience for my stories."

Under the spring sun, the Storyteller breathed in horse sweat and sweet apple blossoms. Ever since he had heard the Kulloo Makoo tell his stories, he had felt a little dizzy, and maybe just a little more daring than usual. All the same, he was afraid of horses, even storytelling ones. He did not answer right away.

"Don't forget I can fly," said the Horse. "It won't be a matter of joggling your brains up and down if that's what you're worried about."

The Storyteller twirled a finger around and around in his beard. Still he did not speak.

"Well," said the Horse. "I'll be off." He switched his tail at the bumblebee and with a rustling of leaves plodded heavily away.

Blue Mountain gleamed in the distance. "There's fishing out there," the Storyteller mused, "and stories," he added, cradling the Story Pouch in his hands. "The fishing would be better if I traveled by boat," he said. "And safer."

"Except for the sharks," murmured the Cat.

"But flying," continued the Storyteller. "Imagine all that soaring and sailing. And the view! Imagine the view!" The Storyteller took a step toward the Horse. "He doesn't seem unfriendly," said the Storyteller. "I mean, I don't think he would just suddenly buck me off or anything."

"You never know, though," said the Cat.

"And," said the Storyteller, taking another step toward the Horse, "flying would be a lot less work than paddling. At least for me." He waved the Story Pouch in the air. "Hold up your horses there, Horse!" he yelled. "I'm coming with you."

"Thought you'd be along," said the Horse, stopping and turning to wait for the Storyteller. He spread his wings. "Make yourself at home."

"That won't be easy," said the Cat, leaping onto the Horse's back, "but don't think you're going without me."

"Ouch," said the Horse. "Pull in your claws, Cat, and hang on, Storyteller. We've got some traveling to do."

3

With a jog, a stride, and then finally a leap, the Horse soared above the trees. The Storyteller buried his face in the Horse's mane, trying to pretend he was home in bed. The Cat, perched behind the Storyteller, bared his fangs at a startled sparrow hawk.

"How do you like it?" asked the Horse, twisting back to look at the Storyteller.

"Ummmmmmmph," said the Storyteller. Slowly he raised his head and looked about. A pond, a blue eye way below in the green, winked up at him. The river unraveled like a silver thread through the green-needled forest. Blue Mountain, a blue giant, gleamed against the horizon.

"I should think the clouds have lots of stories in them," said the Storyteller, leaning back to look up. He gingerly unclasped one hand from the Horse to touch the Talking Bird. "Yes, I have found one about a weasel," he said, trying to open the Story Pouch with his teeth. It slipped from his shoulder.

"Oh no! It's not tied," the Storyteller cried, lunging for it, "and all my stories, and my father's and his father's and *his* father's," he said, falling from the Horse, "will be loooooooooooooooooost!"

Down he went, headfirst, like an overgrown owl swooping for its prey. As the earth rushed up to meet him, there came, not a bone-crushing thud, but a belly-smacking splat. Down went the Storyteller, down to the cold, dark, greasy bottom where river quillworts brushed his face.

"The river!" thought the Storyteller. "Not going to stay here." He kicked and thrashed. "Oooooooof!" he said, exploding out on the bank. "What a terrible experience." He fell into a deep sleep.

"Achoo!" The Storyteller woke up sneezing. A boy with green eyes and skin as pale as the moon was kneeling beside him, blowing dandelion fuzz in his face.

"Achoo! What are you doing?" demanded the Storyteller.

"I am planting dandelions in your beard," said the Boy.

The Storyteller sat up, rubbing his face. The Boy was wearing the Storyteller's hat, and slung over his shoulder was the Story Pouch.

"You haven't, by any chance," asked the Storyteller, "seen a brown leather pouch about—oh—" the Storyteller held up his hands—"this big, have you?"

"A leather pouch," said the pale boy, shaking his head slowly. His green eyes blinked. "Is it like mine?" he asked, holding up the Story Pouch.

"Hmmm, yes," said the Storyteller, "just like yours."

"No, I haven't," said the Boy. "But I found this hat. Is it yours?" he asked, handing the hat to the Storyteller.

"Yes, thank you," said the Storyteller, putting it on. "Do you, by any chance, keep anything in your pouch?" he asked. "My stories, for instance?"

The Boy opened the pouch. "See," he said proudly, "I have a blue heron's feather, strawberries, a toad, and a white stone with a black ring around it."

The Storyteller heaved a deep sigh. "Why haven't the Horse and Cat missed me?" he wondered. "I shall be stranded here forever. The Wise Old Mother will never know I found a

horse, and she'll never, never scold me again." The Storyteller was close to tears. "And if they do find me," he muttered, "I will have dandelions growing in my beard."

"What did you keep in your pouch?" asked the Boy. He stared at the Storyteller with his green eyes. "Did you say stories?"

"Yes, stories," grunted the Storyteller. "And I am going to look for them." He stood up. "How can I pass on my stories if I don't have any stories?" He walked along a path beside the river. The Boy leaped beside him, swinging the pouch in circles over his head.

"Once upon a time," said a crusty voice.

As the Storyteller and the Boy followed a bend in the river, they saw three farmers sitting on stumps. "Once upon a time," said the voice again, coming from a potatoey-looking man who was repairing the end of a hayfork.

"Zzzzzzzzzzzzz," snored a thin, wilted carroty man. He breathed through a gap in his front teeth. His eyelids fluttered over his eyes.

"Anybody got any tobaccer?" yelled a muskmelony man as he knocked his pipe loudly on the side of a stump.

The potatoey man cleared his throat loudly. "Don't you want to hear my story?" he asked.

"Aw, shucks, Spuds," said the muskmelony one. "We know your stories. Look here, you've already put him to sleep and you haven't even told it yet."

"You won't be sorry," said Spuds, potato eyes sparkling. "Once upon a time," he began, although the carroty farmer was still snoring and the Muskmelon was busily cleaning his pipe, "there was a horse who wandered into Farmer Bone's field."

"That's *my* story," cried the Storyteller, starting toward Farmer Spuds.

"Shhh," said the Boy, pulling him back. "I want to hear."

The farmer went on telling the Farmer Bone story, unraveling it word by word. The Carrot opened his eyes wide and sat up straight. The Muskmelon stopped cleaning his pipe and now and then gave a low deep chuckle.

"They are enjoying my story," whispered the Storyteller, pride prickling the back of his neck. "So *this* is why storytellers tell stories."

"And so the story ends," said Farmer Spuds.

"Eh, Spuds," said the Carrot, "that was a good one."

"Guess it's been a while," said the Muskmelon, puffing on his pipe, "since I heard better. Where'd you hear that one, Spuds?"

"I just found it," said Spuds, a shy smile on his knobby face. "Want to hear it again?"

"Guess I could," said the Muskmelon, "only let me tell it this time."

"No, let me," said the Carrot, waving his long bony fingers in the air.

"They're fighting over *my* story," murmured the Storyteller in amazement.

"Do *you* tell stories like that, Storyteller?" asked the Boy, pulling on his arm as they walked away.

"No," said the Storyteller truthfully. "I just collect them. At least I used to. In a pouch. Which I used to own."

The sun was setting. The Storyteller and the Boy cast long shadows as they walked back to the river.

"Do you suppose," mumbled the Storyteller, "I really need the Story Pouch? It's just as easy to remember the stories as pull them out of the pouch. I do not have anyone to pass them on to, and besides, now that I have lost the pouch, I feel more like telling stories than I used to."

"I'm hungry," said the Boy.

"Then go home," said the Storyteller gruffly. "And, anyway," he mumbled again, "I still have the Talking Bird. I can find new stories. And maybe I will tell some of them."

"Don't have a home," said the Boy. He leaped beside the Storyteller. "Walls and floors and roofs make me itch."

The Storyteller sat by the river and rested his head on his knees. He too was hungry. He wished he could fish, but the fishhook had been in the pouch. He wished he had his pipe and his fire. He fell into a hungry sleep. He dreamed the Wise Old Mother was scolding him for losing the porridge.

The Storyteller woke under a black sky to the smell of woodsmoke. The pale face of the Boy glowed as he stirred a black pot over a fire.

"You can have some of my fish stew," said the Boy, "and then you can tell me a story." He handed the Storyteller a spoon.

"Why should I tell you a story?" asked the Storyteller.

"Because I make good fish stew," said the Boy. "Catfish, onions, and dandelion greens. And besides, I like your stories."

"Not bad," said the Storyteller, tasting the stew. "How did you catch the fish?"

"With a fishhook," said the Boy.

"That you found?" suggested the Storyteller.

"Yes," said the Boy, "how did you know that?"

"I just know," said the Storyteller. "How do you know you like my stories?"

"I just know," said the Boy. He crept beside the Storyteller and leaned against him. He smelled of onions and fish, of strawberries and leather pouch.

"Tell me a story," begged the Boy.

"Shhhhh," said the Storyteller. "I have to find one first." He held the Talking Bird against his cheek. He gazed at the fire glowing in the Boy's green eyes. "Hmmmm," he said, "I think I have found one."

Once upon a time [he said], *there was an old, old tree who lived in an old, old forest.*

She was called Grandmother Tree because she was the first tree of the forest and because all things were her children.

The Birds had fallen first as her leaves. Growing wings, they had flown up to build nests in her branches.

From her roots came the Snake.

From her bark came the Bear.

Each season, new creatures were born from some part of the tree.

As she grew, and her bark split and became ragged and

rough, a girl and a boy stepped from the heart of her trunk. Now all the creatures were born—all but one.

Then an acorn fell from Grandmother Tree. It rolled and rolled, gathering mud and sticks and stones. It formed the shape of a Rabbit. Even now, Rabbit has just a little round acorn of a tail. And so the story ends.

"I knew I liked your stories," said the Boy, pulling a handful of squashed strawberries out of the pouch. "Want some?" he asked the Storyteller.

"No, thank you," said the Storyteller, standing. "I think I'll be on my way to Blue Mountain. Since I'm going to have to walk, I had better be going."

"I am coming with you," said the Boy, jumping up.

"You are not coming with me," said the Storyteller. "Boys make me itch."

"You need a boy for telling stories to," said the Boy. The Storyteller began to walk away. "Here, Storyteller," said the Boy. "If you let me come with you, I will let you have my pouch."

The Storyteller put his hat on his head. He stared at the ground, twisting a finger around and around in his beard. "Boy," he said finally, "you keep the pouch for your rocks and things." He looked up, but the Boy had disappeared. The pouch was lying by his feet. The Storyteller sighed, picked it up, and slung it over his shoulder. "Oh well," he said. "The Great-Grandfather would not have wanted me to give it away."

The Storyteller walked along the moonlit river. As he tried to think about all his adventures since he had run away from an evening's scold, he kept being startled by shadows leaping across the water.

"Perhaps I should have let the Boy come with me," said the Storyteller nervously. "After all, he was the first person I ever told a story to, not counting the Kulloo Makoo." A tree on the other side of the river groaned. "Oh, Cat!" cried the Storyteller. "How I wish I had not lost you! Please," he said to the Talking Bird, "help me find some stories to keep me company."

The Storyteller looked, but every story he found was about ghosts or headless men with bloody stumps for hands. "Oh, Talking Bird," whispered the Storyteller, "why are you doing this?" The water lapping against the riverbank answered with a laugh.

"I will sing," said the Storyteller, "to keep away the shudders."

"'Twas a one-eyed fish that did appear," sang the Story-teller, "with a conch shell in his fin."

There was a splashing on the river just behind the Story-teller. "Hmmmm," he said, without turning to look, "some-thing seems to be following me. I will sing even louder and maybe it will go away." Drawing a deep breath, the Story-teller sang, "'There's a snail, a snail, a snail,' cried the fish, 'and he's a-drawing neeeear, and he's a-drawing neeeeeear!'"

The Storyteller's singing was more like shouting. Even so, he could not fool the splashing sound out of his ears.

"Storyteller!" a voice called. "I found your hat. It fell off while you were walking."

Right beside the Storyteller on the river was the Boy. He was sitting in a bark canoe with a paddle across his knees.

"Oh," said the Storyteller. He put a hand to his heart. "It's you." He took the hat and fanned his face. "Where did you get that boat? I suppose you found that too?"

"Yes, I did," said the Boy, blinking his green eyes.

The Storyteller twirled his finger in his beard. "If you'd like," he said, "you can give me a ride in your boat."

"I'd like to very much," said the Boy. "I just happen to have also found two paddles. Where would you like to go?" he

46

asked, as the Storyteller carefully climbed into the canoe.

"I would like to go to Blue Mountain," said the Storyteller. "But perhaps you are not going that way?" he added politely.

"It just happens I *was* going to Blue Mountain," said the Boy, leaning forward and digging his paddle into the water. "Perhaps you could find me a story or two on the way?"

"I don't know," said the Storyteller, looking doubtfully at the Talking Bird. "It might not be one you will want to hear."

The Storyteller looked for a moment at the Boy's pale face. It was a small mysterious moon.

"I have found a story," cried the Storyteller, "and it is not a fearsome one. Now, Pouch," he said, opening it up. "Here is a new story for you."

Once upon a time [he said], *the moon laughed like a loon when the sun went down.*

All the animals knew then that the season had turned, and by the next moon they must be prepared to journey or sleep or hunt—all but Rabbit, who preferred to play and did not want Winter to come that year.

Rabbit jumped up to the tallest ice hill. "If I can see the Ice King," he said, "maybe I can put him off for a moon or two."

And there he was, hoarfrost for hair and icicles for a beard. He was way away, but he was striding mightily, turning the earth white as he came on.

"I know what to do," said clever young Rabbit.

With a flick of his tail, he ran up north. With a scrape here and a slap there, he made the handsomest Ice Queen there ever was.

His paws did get frosty, but Rabbit rode on the Ice Queen's shoulders until they met up with the Ice King. As soon as he saw her, the King forgot where he was going. That King and Queen stayed right where they were. First they played, taking turns making blizzards. Then they rested for a while, the Queen singing to the King, while her hair, made of ice crystals, blew in the breeze and made a music of its own.

Rabbit ran home and for another two moons there was no Winter.

The trouble was, the Ice Queen melted. Bit by bit, you understand, so the Ice King's heart nearly melted too.

Winter came late that year, but when it did come, it was the worst for ice and storming that anyone could ever remember.

And so the story ends.

"That was one of the best stories I've found in a long time," said the Storyteller, happily trailing a hand in the water. "The Wise Old Mother was right. What my storytelling needed was some traveling."

"Ha," said the Boy. "More likely what you needed was a boy. Come on, Storyteller, paddle. You're making me do all the work."

4

The Storyteller and the Boy traveled up the river. They fished when they were hungry, slept on the mossy bank when they were tired, and all the while the Storyteller collected stories.

"Tell me a story," said the Boy every evening after a meal of wild parsley and pickerel or of trout and pepper-cap mushrooms. Every evening the Storyteller told the Boy the best story he had found that day, until, finally, they reached Blue Lake, and on its far side, Blue Mountain.

"At last," said the Storyteller, rocking the canoe in excitement.

The Boy dipped his paddle in Blue Lake, ruffling the reflection of the mountain.

"There are stories up there," said the Storyteller, looking up, "such as are not found anywhere else in the land."

"How do you know?" asked the Boy. He paddled to the beach at the edge of the lake.

"I know because I am a storyteller," said the Storyteller. "But I wonder how we get up there."

"Look," said the Boy, leaping from the canoe. "You see how that path goes through the field into the woods? I expect that is the way up Blue Mountain."

"I expect you are right," said the Storyteller.

They beached the canoe, and the Storyteller strode quickly across the field.

"You are lucky to have a boy to tell you these things," said the Boy, running after him. "But slow down, Storyteller, I cannot keep up with you."

The Storyteller did not hear, for as he entered the woods, he found stories all about him. They unfurled in wispy curls from the birches. They sang in the song of the white-throated sparrow. They hung in the scent of the pines, and where streams muddied the path, they oozed between his toes.

"Thank you, Talking Bird," said the Storyteller, kissing the circle, "but I will not stop to collect stories here, for the very best ones will be at the top."

"Aren't we there yet?" grumbled the Boy after several hours of climbing.

"Here we are," said the Storyteller as they finally reached the rocky summit. "Look," he said. He pointed across an ocean of forest. "Way, way over there the Wise Old Mother is sweeping the cabin, scolding the dust for daring to settle on the floor."

"Probably not the dust the Wise Old Mother is scolding," said a familiar voice. The Storyteller looked about uncomfortably. The Cat appeared from behind a rock. "Probably it is a certain person the Wise Old Mother is scolding. Wake up, Horse," he said. "Look who's here."

"I thought I would never see you again," said the Storyteller, kneeling happily to the Cat. "And there is the Horse!"

"You disappeared into thin air," said the Cat gruffly. "Storytellers aren't supposed to fly. Neither are horses. Wake up, Horse."

"Well, well, well," said the Horse. He unbuckled his legs. "The Storyteller and a boy."

"I found him," said the Boy proudly, "and I gave him my pouch because he lost his."

"I found the Woodcarver," said the Horse, standing slowly. "Oooof. I am getting stiff from all my exertions. First I bring the Cat up here to look for voles, and then off I go for a little sightseeing. And then I am pulled into the biggest apple tree in the land between the Sea and Blue Mountain. The Woodcarver's hut was right next to it. Ahhhh," said the Horse, sniffing. "Good mountain air."

"Did you ask the Woodcarver about your wings?" asked the Storyteller.

"She told me I had a choice," said the Horse. "If I didn't want apple, I could have chestnut, cherry, or hop hornbeam. I said, 'What about *real* wings?' and she said, 'Some beasts are too greedy for their own good.'"

"Ha," said the Cat.

"She said she is a woodcarver," continued the Horse, "and she only works in wood, not feathers and bone."

"Speaking of bone," said the Cat, "excuse me." He crouched as a vole ran by on skittery legs.

"Poor vole," cried the Boy as the Cat's paw darted out.

"Poor Cat!" cried the Storyteller. "Look at that vole! It's

getting bigger and bigger! Cat!" called the Storyteller. "Stay away!"

"The vole is a mole!" squeaked the Cat. He ducked, but too late. The creature swatted him with a shovelly paw.

"That's re*vole*ting," said the Horse, nervously laughing his carrot-munching laugh.

The mole raised its head, chuckled long and loud, and lumbered to the edge of the mountain, where it disappeared.

The Storyteller shuddered to hear a laughing mole. "Poor Cat," he said, kneeling to comfort him. "How were you to know Blue Mountain voles turn into giant moles?"

"And Blue Mountain used to be a *vole*cano," said the Horse. "Har har."

"Leave me alone," growled the Cat, limping away.

"Enough excitement for one day," said the Horse. "Wake me when you want to leave." He stretched behind a rock and went to sleep.

The Storyteller held up the Talking Bird and began to look for stories. In a lichen-covered boulder, he found the Wind Bird and the Fox. In a cloud shadow, he found the Skunk and the Oak Leaf.

"Here, Boy," said the Storyteller. "I have found a story in

this twisted little tree that I think you will like. Come and listen."

Once upon a time [said the Storyteller], *the Boy, who had lived in the forest all his life, wanted to see the World. He went to Grandmother Tree and asked her what he should do.*

"Where do you want to go?" she asked.

"To the highest place in the World," said the Boy.

"For those who live in the western canyons, this is the highest place in the World," said Grandmother Tree. "Where else do you want to go?"

"To the lowest place in the World," said the Boy.

"For those who live in the eastern mountains, this is the lowest place in the World," said Grandmother Tree. "Where else do you want to go?"

"To the coldest place in the World," said the Boy.

"For those who live in the southern desert, this is the coldest place in the World," said Grandmother Tree. "Where else do you want to go?"

"To the hottest place in the World," said the Boy.

"For those who live in the northern ice fields, this is the hottest place in the World," said Grandmother Tree. "Is there any-

where else you would like to go?"

"Where no one has ever been before," said the Boy.

"Ah," said Grandmother Tree. "Then you had better climb to the very top of my branches, where no one has ever been before."

The Boy climbed up into Grandmother Tree, climbing branch after branch, until he was at the top where no one had ever been before. To the west he saw canyons; to the east, mountains. To the south he saw desert; to the north, ice fields.

The Boy climbed down, satisfied he had been where no one had ever been before.

And so the story ends.

"That is a good story," said the Boy. "If I had not been with you, I am sure you would not have found it."

"Next I expect you will tell me I do not need the Talking Bird anymore," said the Storyteller, laughing. He looped the Story Pouch to his belt. "I have found enough stories today. Let us sleep on the mountain and tomorrow I will look for more."

The Boy gathered sticks to build a fire for roasting the asparagus ferns he had collected on the way up. The sun was beginning to set, smoothing the cragged edges of the mountain. The trees on the ridges turned purple. In the valley, the forest deepened to a black-green. As the sun disappeared, the mountain turned blue.

"I hope the Cat returns soon," said the Storyteller.

"Tell one more story," pleaded the Boy. "Perhaps the Cat will come back by the time you have finished it."

"One more story," said the Storyteller, staring into the fire. "I think I see one about Fire-eyed Birds."

"I don't know if I want to hear that one," said the Boy, moving closer to the Storyteller.

"Listen," said the Storyteller. "The Woodcarver is in it."

Once upon a time [said the Storyteller], *the Woodcarver lived in a hut under densely woven laurel branches. She lived alone, enjoying the company of creatures carved from wood. Although she was the master of her craft, one day she found great difficulty carving a certain bird. Just when she carved the last feather, she grew displeased with it. "No," she would cry, tossing bird after bird into the fire, "that is not how it should be done at all." She did not know that as she worked, the unfinished birds were sparked into life by the fire. As they grew in size, their rage magnified when they perceived they were unfinished. Flames danced in the eyes of wood that did not burn, and yet a smoke filled the Woodcarver's hut. At last she turned to discover what monsters they had become.*

"Storyteller," said the Boy, tugging on the Storyteller's sleeve.

The Woodcarver rushed from the hut, running before the wooden wings that thrashed the air into a wind.

"Storyteller," cried the Boy, jumping up, "do you hear that wind?"

"You must never interrupt a storyteller," said the Storyteller, catching the Boy's leg.

"But, Storyteller," said the Boy struggling free, "do you hear that wind?"

"I do not need a boy," said the Storyteller, shaking a fist at the Boy, "who cannot sit still and listen."

"But, Storyteller," shouted the Boy, "my eyes are burning."

"For the last time—" threatened the Storyteller.

"JUMP ON!" cried the Horse. The air thrummed with the beating of wings. Flaming eyes kindled the darkness. Something hard brushed against the Storyteller's face.

"Jump on!" shouted the Horse again. "There is no time to lose." He lunged off the side of the mountain.

"Oh, Cat, where are you?" wailed the Storyteller. He flung one arm about the Horse's neck, pulling the Boy along with the other. They dropped through black air, the raging birds screaming after them.

"I must tell the end of the story," gasped the Storyteller. "I must finish what the Woodcarver began."

"What are you saying?" cried the Boy, his arms grasped tightly around the Storyteller's neck. "I cannot hear you."

The Storyteller shouted his words to the darkness.

The Woodcarver ran from the birds, and just as she thought she could no longer fend them off, a horse appeared. He frightened them away just long enough for her to fashion him a pair of wings so he could lead the birds from her. This he did, taking them to Blue Mountain. Away from the Woodcarver, the birds forgot their anger and fell asleep. They did not wake until roused by the Storyteller's story. Once more they attacked. The Storyteller and the Boy and the Horse—(the Cat was lost)—fled into the night, but the birds pursued, getting closer and closer and CLOSER. The Storyteller knew if he could finish the story, they would be saved.

"Hurry," said the Horse, "my tail is getting singed."

"Hurry," said the Horse, "my tail is getting singed" [continued the Storyteller].

"I am so tired," groaned the Boy. "I do not think I can hang on for another minute."

And the Boy said, "I am so tired—

"STORYTELLER!" cried the Horse. "If you are going to finish the story, finish it!"

"I am trying to," said the Storyteller, "but you keep adding to it."

Just as the Horse thought he could go no further, the flames grew brighter and the air crackled with heat.

"They are burning us!" shouted the Boy. "Help! I do not like being in a story."

The smoke came billowing in great clouds. The Storyteller and the Boy and the Horse thought all was lost.

"I can't breathe," choked the Horse.

Back at the laurel hut, the Woodcarver gave one last flick of her knife. "There, I am done," she said proudly. She placed the finished carving of the bird on the mantel above her fireplace.

The screaming of the Fire-eyed Birds stopped.

"What happened?" asked the Horse, so startled he stopped flying for a moment. "It is so quiet."

Crackling fireballs whizzed past the Horse and his companions. They fell far, far below, leaving trails of light like shooting stars. The Fire-eyed Birds were gone.

"It worked, Storyteller!" shouted the Boy. "And so the story ends," he added, kicking his heels into the Horse's sides.

"Not quite," said the Horse, flapping his wings wildly.

"Fly, Horse, use your wings," urged the Storyteller, as faster and faster they fell. The wind rushed up, whipping the Horse's tail into the Storyteller's face.

"We must be over an apple tree," said the Horse. "There is nothing I can do. Just hang on and you will be all right."

Down, down they fell, down into the limbs of an apple tree, where broken twigs scraped the Storyteller's face.

"Ugh," said the Horse. "I think I am apple-plectic."

"Now the story ends," said the Boy, who was hanging upside down, "if we can ever get out of this tree. Can you tell a story about that, Storyteller?"

The Storyteller did not answer. The only sound was a stirring of leaves as the Storyteller tried to twist a finger around and around in his beard.

"I will never tell another story," wailed the Storyteller.

"Oh, no," said the Boy. "Why not?"

The Storyteller broke through the branches and fell to the ground. "The Talking Bird," he said. Tears came to his eyes. "My father's, and his father's, and *his* father's Talking Bird. I have lost it," he said, banging his head on the ground. "For once and for all, I am not a storyteller and never will be."

"Oh, no," said the Boy as he crashed beside the Storyteller, "and this time I don't think I can find another one for you."

5

The Storyteller fell asleep. He dreamed his mother had fire eyes.

"Wake up, Horse," said the Storyteller when the sun came up. "We must follow the river to find our way back to the mountain. I cannot go home without the Cat."

"We cannot go back to the mountain," said the Horse without opening his eyes.

"Whyever not?" asked the Storyteller.

"The Woodcarver lives below the mountain, and she will find out," said the Horse.

"She will find out what?" asked the Storyteller impatiently.

"She will find out I led the Fire-eyed Birds to the mountain. She said, on that fateful day when I first met her, 'Lead them away,' and it turns out I led them right above her house where they could have descended in incendiary flight, destroying her in a wondrous blaze."

"I don't see that it is your fault," said the Storyteller, putting on his hat. "You did not know her house was below the mountain. And I think they might have slept forever if I had not awakened them by mentioning the Woodcarver's name."

The Horse opened his old bark-colored eyes. "Of course," he said. "She ought to be grateful I led them away at all." He stretched one leg at a time before standing. "Storyteller, since you have given up storytelling, you should go in for cheering up folks. After all, one storyteller amongst us is probably enough."

"Um," said the Storyteller. "But I was beginning to like my stories."

"Of course you were," said the Horse in a nasal tone of voice, as if he were at the end of a neigh, "but let us collect the Boy and be off before I fall back to sleep."

The Storyteller scrambled up on the Horse's back. "Where is the Boy?" he asked. "I have not seen him this morning."

"Where are my wings?" asked the Horse, straining to look at his back. "My wings are missing."

"Watch out below!" a voice screamed. There followed a spluttering of leaves, twigs, and broken branches.

"Poor apple tree," said the Storyteller. He jumped off the Horse and helped the Boy.

"Poor wings," said the Horse.

"Poor *me*," said the Boy, covered with scratches. "I hope I never find another pair of wings as long as I live."

"Huh," grunted the Horse. "I suppose they were just lying around on my back when you found them."

"Come on," said the Storyteller impatiently. He reharnessed the wings to the Horse. "I want to find the Cat and go home. The Wise Old Mother will be wondering where we are. I wonder how long it will be before she discovers I am not a storyteller anymore." He sighed. "I wonder if she ever thought I *was* a storyteller."

Over the thread of river they flew, low enough so they could look for the Cat. Whitecaps raced on the water after the shadow of the Horse.

"Brace yourselves," cried the Horse. "We're over the Woodcarver's tree."

"No Cat," said the Storyteller sadly as he pulled himself out

of the tree, "but there is the Woodcarver's hut.

"There must be a door here somewhere," said the Story-teller. He searched through a tangle of leaves and the pink-white flowers of laurel.

"Here it is," cried the Boy. "I found it!"

The Woodcarver came to the door. She held a bone knife in a hand that was as brown and twisted as an old root. Her skin shone like polished chestnut. "Oh," she said to the Horse in a deep husky voice. "You're back. Something else you don't like about your wings?"

"I have brought a storyteller who is looking for his cat, and a boy," said the Horse, rolling his old bark-colored eyes, "who finds things."

"How useful," said the Woodcarver. She smiled, showing a row of wooden teeth. The front two had knots in them. "I also have lost a cat. I had one this morning and now he has gone. Perhaps the Boy can find both of them. Come in," she said, gesturing with her knife. "I will show you the carving I am making of my cat."

"I will go look for your cats," said the Boy. He leaped into the woods.

"Being under a roof makes him itch," said the Storyteller.

He followed the Woodcarver into the hut.

The Horse stood outside but pushed his head through a small round window.

Inside, a fire burned in a stone fireplace. A carved wooden bird perched on the mantel, its feathers and tail, eyes and beak formed perfectly. Wood shavings littered the floor. Wooden figures looked down from shelves that lined the walls.

"Look!" cried the Storyteller, stumbling toward a shelf. "There is Grandmother Tree," he said, pointing, "and the Wind Bird and the Fox, the Skunk and the Oak Leaf, and," he said, turning to the bird on the mantel and shuddering, "the Fire-eyed Birds. Where did you find these?"

"Why," said the Woodcarver in her husky voice, "I see their shapes and carve them from wood. That is why I am a woodcarver."

"And I see them and tell a story about them. That is why I am a storyteller," said the Storyteller, forgetting for the moment he no longer was one.

"Then do tell one!" cried the Woodcarver, waving her knife in the air. "Here," she said, taking up a figure. "Tell the Bent Old Woman. She is one of my favorites." The bend in the old woman's back came from a twist in a maple branch. She carried a maple cane in one hand, and a basket woven of spider grass in the other.

The Storyteller stood in a corner of the room. He twisted a finger around and around in his beard. "That is a story I have not yet found," he said.

"So much the better," said the Woodcarver. "How exciting to find it now!"

"I cannot tell the story," said the Storyteller softly.

"Do not be bashful," said the Woodcarver. She reached for a wooden bottle and a wooden cup from one of the shelves. "Sit down, Storyteller, and refresh yourself with Blue Mountain blueberry wine while you tell the story."

The Storyteller sat in a chair and twisted his hat around and around.

"I cannot tell the story," he said again.

The Woodcarver flashed her woody smile. "It is really most kind of you to not want to upset me," she said, sitting in another chair. She placed the Bent Old Woman on the table in front of the Storyteller. "Please understand I do not mind you finding stories for my figures."

The Storyteller flung his hat on the floor. "I do not have a story about a bent old woman. Ask me for another story. How about the Skunk and the Oak Leaf? That's a good one."

"I do not want to hear about the Skunk and the Oak Leaf," said the Woodcarver. Her voice deepened into a growl. "I want to hear about the Bent Old Woman."

"He can't tell it," snorted the Horse from the window. "He's lost his Talking Bird. That wooden thing he wore around his neck that found his stories for him."

"What?" cried the Woodcarver, standing. She rapped a rooty hand under the Storyteller's nose. "And you call yourself a storyteller?"

"I do not know what else to call myself," said the Storyteller, hanging his head.

"Hem, hem," said the Horse. His jowls sagged over the windowsill. "You may have noticed I tell stories and *I* do not have a talking bird."

"A true storyteller," said the Woodcarver, turning her back to the Storyteller. She placed her chair near the window. "Do begin, Storyteller," she said to the Horse. "I want to hear about the Bent Old Woman." She took up the carving of the cat and began to shape his tail.

"The Bent Old Woman," said the Horse, chewing thoughtfully on his lower lip. "Yes. I have a *bent* for telling stories, don't you know?"

"No, I don't," muttered the Storyteller. He sat hunched in his chair and kicked the table. "I'm just as good a storyteller as he ever was."

"Pay no attention," said the Woodcarver to the Horse. "Do begin, please."

The Horse half shut his old bark-colored eyes. "It all began in a meadow," he said. "A modest little meadow with sweet vernal grass and lovely pale-violet-blue cranesbill. Under an apple tree, a horse was born. How well he remembered his mother's gentle nosing as she urged him to stand for the first time."

The Woodcarver looked up from her carving. "When do we get to the Bent Old Woman?" she asked.

"In due time," said the Horse. "I am setting the scene."

"The Kulloo Makoo liked my stories," said the Storyteller under his breath, "and the farmers, and the Boy. The Boy especially," he said. He gazed at the fire, remembering the stories he had told by the river. "And *I* liked my stories, I really did," he continued, a prickle of pride bringing tears to his eyes.

"Horse," said the Woodcarver, "do get on with it."

"Once upon a time," said the Storyteller, straightening in his chair.

"I beg your pardon?" said the Woodcarver. "Do you always interrupt other people when they are telling stories?"

"Did you say 'Once upon a time'?" asked the Storyteller.

"No," said the Woodcarver. "*You* did. Very rude too."

Once upon a time there was a girl who lived with her deaf and dumb mother in a hut in a forest.

The Storyteller spoke very quickly, slurring his words together. Springing from the chair, he picked up the Bent Old Woman. "Did I just say something again or was that the Horse?" he asked.

"That was you," said the Woodcarver, "and if you don't stop interrupting, I am going to have to ask you to leave."

The Storyteller held the Bent Old Woman in both hands.

The girl loved her mother, but sometimes she thought she would lose the use of her own voice, for there was never anyone to talk to.

One day as the girl was walking in the forest, she met a bent old woman gathering sticks.

"The Bent Old Woman!" cried the Woodcarver. She turned her chair to face the Storyteller again, put down her knife, and clasped her long fingers together.

"I was just getting to her," complained the Horse, snorting as he stamped outside the window.

So happy was she to see another person [continued the Storyteller], *she ran to help the woman.*

"For your kindness to me," said the woman when the basket was full, "take this stick and burn it not." She turned and hobbled away.

As the girl held the stick, her ears were filled with a strange sound, and strange words formed on her tongue. She soon realized that the stick helped her to understand and talk to the birds. She chattered with them happily all the rest of that day and for many days to come.

One day she was laughing with a jay when a young man came walking toward her. She could see he was moving his lips, but she could not understand him until she put down the stick. Then she heard him say, "How pretty you are!"

The young man returned the next day, and the next. He became a friend to the girl and to the girl's mother.

One evening the girl held the stick and told the birds of her joy, for the young man had asked her to marry.

The Bent Old Woman drew near. "I will take back the stick now," she whispered in her old voice, "for now that love is speaking, there is no need to be listening to birds."

Sadly, the girl returned the stick, but at the same time she heard her young man calling her. She was soon happy again, but to show she had not forgotten her friends, her first-born she named "Jay," and her second-born "Robin."

"And so the story ends," said the Storyteller. He sank into a chair. Trembling, he looked at the Woodcarver. "Tell me the truth, Woodcarver," he said. "Did I just find a story, all by myself, without the Talking Bird?"

"Ah," said the Woodcarver. She raised a glass of Blue Mountain blueberry wine. "Storyteller, you are a storyteller after all."

The Horse coughed from the window. "Wondrous bad taste, if you ask me. I thought you said you needed that wooden thing to tell your stories." He started to back out of the window. "You were trying to make a fool of me, Story-teller."

"Hold your horses, there, Horse," said the Storyteller. He walked to the window and scratched the Horse between his ears. "Of course I thought I needed the Talking Bird. Until now, I have not been able to find a story without it."

"You did not have to find this out in the middle of *my* story," grumbled the Horse.

"Horse!" cried the Storyteller, kissing him on the nose. "Don't you see? You were talking away, and *I* so much wanted to tell the story of the Bent Old Woman. And I thought of it, I did," shouted the Storyteller, "without the Talking Bird! I don't need it anymore, or maybe," he added, looking startled, "I never did. The question is, did my great-grandfather know that? And my grandfather? And," said the Storyteller, shaking his head in amazement, "my father?"

"Tell me," said the Woodcarver, opening a wooden chest and taking out a wooden box, "was the Talking Bird carved on a piece of oak?"

"Yes, it was," said the Storyteller.

"And was it rather like a heron with a tufty head and a graceful neck and a wide-open bill?"

"Yes," said the Storyteller. "Have you seen it?"

"I have seen these," said the Woodcarver. She scooped a handful of wooden circles from the box. "My great-grandmother carved them," she said, holding one out for the Storyteller. "They were her buttons."

"Buttons!" exclaimed the Storyteller, taking one. He traced

his fingers over the carving of the bird. "Buttons," he muttered.

"You may keep it if you like," said the Woodcarver. "Perhaps it will help you find your cat."

The door opened. The Boy stayed outside as the Cat ambled indoors. "I only found one of the cats," he said.

"He is *my* Cat," said the Storyteller and the Woodcarver at the same time.

"Truth is," muttered the Cat, "*he* belongs to *me*." He sat down beside the Storyteller.

"Oh," said the Woodcarver with her woody smile. "I guess I *used* to have a cat."

"Boy," said the Storyteller. He unlooped the Story Pouch from his belt, "after all these days of traveling together, I have come to see that you are right. I do need a boy."

"Of course you do," said the Boy from the doorway, although his green eyes turned a deeper green.

"I need a boy," said the Storyteller, "to pass on, as my father did, and his father, and *his* father, the Story Pouch, and," he said, holding out the Great-Grandmother's button, "the Talking Bird. Now you can begin to learn how to be a storyteller."

The Boy's moon face beamed like a sun. He took the Story Pouch and the button from the Storyteller, "But, Storyteller," he said, "I thought you lost the Talking Bird."

"I was mistaken," said the Storyteller. "By a lucky accident, it fell into the Story Pouch."

"I will let you use it whenever you want to find a story," said the Boy. "*I'm* already good at finding things. I should be good at finding stories."

But how long will it be, thought the Storyteller, *before he finds the secret of the Talking Bird?* "Now Horse," he said, gently nudging the Horse, who was asleep and snoring with his head still in the window, "the Wise Old Mother will be in a dithering scold by this time. Let us be off."

The Woodcarver shook a rooty hand with the Storyteller. "Come back," she said. "I shall have carved more figures and I would like to hear their stories."

"I shall have told more stories," said the Storyteller. He walked out of the hut. "I would like to see who is in them. Good-bye, Woodcarver," he said, climbing up on the Horse. The Boy and the Cat leaped up behind him.

"Good-bye, Horse," said the Woodcarver. "Come back if you need a new pair of wings. I have not forgotten you saved my life."

"I should hope not," said the Horse, spreading his wings. He sprang into the air. The Woodcarver and the hut grew smaller and smaller. Soon even Blue Mountain hung like a memory on the horizon.

"Do you suppose," whispered the Storyteller into the Horse's mane, "that my father and his father and *his* father before him passed on the Talking Bird when they discovered they could find their stories without it? And," he added, squeezing his eyes shut with delight, "the Wise Old Mother never even knew!"

"Hang on!" cried the Horse.

Down, down they fell into the arms of the old apple tree where the Storyteller had first met the Horse.

The Storyteller gazed at the stone wall and the old, old forest where the trees were tall and thick trunked.

"At last we are home," said the Storyteller. He unhooked himself from a branch.

The Horse thudded to the ground. "Oooof. I am getting too old for this."

"I am getting too old for a scold," said the Storyteller. He walked slowly toward the cabin.

The door to the cabin opened. "I see you have decided to come home," said the Wise Old Mother. She shook her corn-

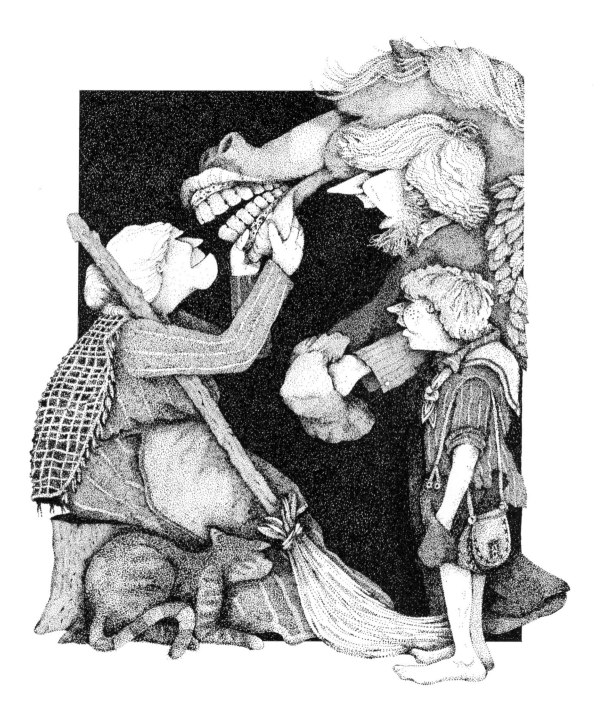

husk broom at the Storyteller. "Just in time," she said, her mouth curving down with frown wrinkles. "This very minute I was throwing out your tobacco. And you, Cat," she said, pointing the broom at him, "I suppose your excuse is that you have been off vole hunting?"

"Look, Mother," said the Storyteller, "I have found a horse. And a boy."

The Wise Old Mother raked the Horse over with her wise old eyes. "Speckled gums," she said, opening his mouth.

"Of course," said the Horse. "What did you ex*speck*, har har."

The Wise Old Mother squinted at the Boy. "Thieving eyes," she said.

"I *find* things," said the Boy, pink showing in his pale cheeks. "Here," he said, digging into a pocket, "I found you a carving of the Cat."

The Wise Old Mother fixed her eyes on the Storyteller. She drew in a deep scolding breath. She leaned her broom carefully on the side of the cabin so she could plump her hands on her hips. Wide, wide her mouth opened, in order to push out words to hit the Storyteller.

"Once upon a time," said the Storyteller before her words

could come out. He took the Wise Old Mother firmly by the hand and led her inside the cabin. He took up his pipe and sank into his favorite chair. The Cat settled beside the fireplace. Even the Boy came inside and sat at the Storyteller's feet. Outside, the Horse grazed contentedly on the Wise Old Mother's herbs.

"Once upon a time," said the Storyteller again, and the Wise Old Mother was so surprised to see and hear him tell stories, and such good ones too, that she forgot to scold for a long, long time.

AND SO THE STORY ENDS